Samuel French Acting Edition

No More Sad Things

by Hansol Jung

SAMUELFRENCH.COM   SAMUELFRENCH.CO.UK

FOR PRODUCTION ENQUIRIES

UNITED STATES AND CANADA
Info@SamuelFrench.com
1-866-598-8449

UNITED KINGDOM AND EUROPE
Plays@SamuelFrench.co.uk
020-7255-4302

Each title is subject to availability from Samuel French, depending upon country of performance. Please be aware that *NO MORE SAD THINGS* may not be licensed by Samuel French in your territory. Professional and amateur producers should contact the nearest Samuel French office or licensing partner to verify availability.

MUSIC USE NOTE

IMPORTANT BILLING AND CREDIT REQUIREMENTS

NO MORE SAD THINGS had its co-world premiere production presented by Sideshow Theatre Company at the Biograph Theatre in Chicago, Illinois in November 2015. The performance was directed by Elly Green, with sets by William Boles, lighting by Diane Fairchild, costumes by Izumi Inaba, and sound design by Christopher M. LaPorte. The Stage Manager was Elyse Estes. The cast was as follows:

JESSIEE . . . . Katy Carolina Collins

KAHEKILI . . . . George Infantado

GUIDEBOOK . . . . Narciso Lobo

NO MORE SAD THINGS had its co-world premiere production presented by the Boise Contemporary Theatre in Boise, Idaho in November 2015. The performance was directed by Julie Ritchie, with scenic design and lighting design by Rick Martin, costumes by Hannah Read Newbill, and sound design by Peter John Still. The Stage Manager was Sarah Kelso and the Dramaturg was Whitney Dibo. The cast was as follows:

JESSIEE . . . . Carie Kawa

KAHEKILI . . . . Kaimana Ramos

GUIDEBOOK . . . . Brian Quijada

Additional development venue: Seven Devils Playwright Conference in McCall, Idaho.

CHARACTERS

JESSIEE – Female, thirty-two years old. Any ethnicity.
KAHEKILI – Male, fifteen years old. Hawaiian.
GUIDEBOOK – A guide through things. Any ethnicity.

SETTING

Maui, Ka'anapali Beach

TIME

Now

AUTHOR'S NOTES

(–): a cut-off either by self or other.
(,): at end of a line marks an interruption of thought by another character, not necessarily a line cut-off.
(/): a point where another character might cut in.
New paragraph: a switch of thought
[ ]: things that aren't spoken in words

Original songs by Hansol Jung and Jongbin Jung.
It would be nice if **GUIDEBOOK** plays Polynesian drums and ukulele, and has a lovely voice.

TRANSLATIONS

huhu: angry
honu: turtle
haole: foreigner
lolo: crazy
ule: penis
chiho: expression of total excitement
kahuna: priest, sorcerer
hele mai: come here

*(A **BOY** with an ukulele.)*

*(He is a metaphorical **GUIDEBOOK**.)*

(A hello.)

(He sings a Hawaiian song, something like the first two verses of "Malie's Song" by Keali'I Reichel.*)

GUIDEBOOK.

This is a song. A Hawaiian Song, or [**name of song**].

This is an instrument. Ukulele, or Hawaiian interpretation of the Portugese cavaquinho.

This is a stage. Theatrical Space, or our collective deep dark weird dreams.

(Music ends.)

Welcome.

JESSIEE. I have a dream.

Frogs. Thousands of them all over the house, croaking jumping laying eggs in the kitchen sink.

I'm terrified I hate frogs who doesn't hate frogs?

So I call the frog killing people – hello please I have frogs I want them gone

and they come in with these huge pliers I'm talking massive six-foot-tall men with six-foot-tall pliers they start snipping away at the frogs, snip, snip, snip, with the control of Mister Miyagi from *Karate Kid,*

you know, shnip,

---

*A license to produce *No More Sad Things* does not include a performance license for "Malie's Song." The publisher and author suggest that the licensee contact ASCAP or BMI to ascertain the music publisher and contact such music publisher to license or acquire permission for performance of the song. If a license or permission is unattainable for "Malie's Song," the licensee may not use the song in *No More Sad Things* but may create an original composition in a similar style. For further information, please see Music Use Note on page 3.

hai, super chopsticks!

then back to noodles.

Hours and hours they snip away at my house and then finally they shake my hand and announce:

GUIDEBOOK. "Congratulations, your house is sterile, we will now take our pay."

JESSIEE. In a flash the pliers turn into giant forks and they fork away all of my furniture. All of it, the table, the bed, the little Russian dolls with toothpicks in their heads –

So I'm left in this sterile house, with Nothing left in it, the walls are barely standing.

Then I hear, this little,

GUIDEBOOK. Ribbit. Ribbit.

JESSIEE. I follow the sound,

GUIDEBOOK. Ribbit ribbit.

JESSIEE. It's coming from inside my bathroom.

I'm like, ho, got you now sucker.

Bam, swing open the door and yah! Sure enough,

GUIDEBOOK. Ribbit ribbit ribbit ribbit.

JESSIEE. There he is, a little tadpole stuck to the wall of my toilet bowl.

Our eyes meet.

No one breathes.

Then he grows legs and arms and he's a friggin' frog in two seconds!

I get an urge, a massive six-foot-tall plier urge to squash it, but when I reach out my hands the little thing starts singing.

Yah, singing! In perfect John Denveresque croony tenor he goes,

GUIDEBOOK.

LET ME KNOW YOUR EYES, WARM AS THE SUN
MOLD YOUR SECRETS, DEEP AS YOUR HEART
TRACE YOUR LIPS, TILL NIGHT TURNS TO MORNING

DON'T NEED A LOT
LET ME BE PART OF YOUR BODY

JESSIEE. – Jumps on to my index finger – the one that was about to squash him –

and the little thing chirps in his little frog voice,

GUIDEBOOK. "Bye Mommy,

I'm not mad you had to kill me.

Come find me in Maui."

KAHEKILI. I have dis dream,

eva since I can remember.

Dis lady, yah, sitting on da shore.

She lift up her eyes, an' stay on my eyes, li'dat a long long time like she t'ink I know her, like she want that I know her.

But I'm jus',

I don't.

I want fo' say sumt'ing,

"Hello, who are you, can I help you?"

But I open my mout', an' not'ing come out.

Usually, y'know, I got dis loud talk nobody not hear my talk, my fadda say all da time –

GUIDEBOOK. "Kahekili, you wen gone swallowed da thunder, boy, when you gon' / learn fo' whisper like da kine normal people?"

KAHEKILI. Learn fo' whisper like da kine normal people yadda yadda ya…

But in dis dream, no way dis mout' gon' sound.

Den dis lady she get angry or jus' bored I don know,

but she leave my eyes, walk into da watah an' tek off,

An' I stand stuck in da sand, li'dat stuck in da sand wid dis stupid silent mout',

jus' watchin' dis lady's head up an' down up an' down,

jus' watchin' da waves, da breaks, eat her up

Dass when I hear it.

Dis voice, song, sumt'ing, I hear it go,

GUIDEBOOK. "Psst. Psst psst."

KAHEKILI. I look around, li'dat, li'dat,
    den da sound again,

GUIDEBOOK. "Psst psst. Psst psst."

KAHEKILI. I'm still like, huh? An' den da buggah go,

GUIDEBOOK. "Psst. Kahekili."

KAHEKILI. I look up, an' up deh da most biggest star, neh,
    she blink blink psst psst gon' crazy li'dat.

    Dis my dream, y'know so I can da kine, fly,

    I fly fly fly not like da Superman but like da watahman
    on da breaks,

    fly fly fly.

    Den just when I get up deh, close enough fo' some talk
    dis buggah sings.

    Outta da blue li'dat da buggah sings,

GUIDEBOOK.

    LET ME KNOW YOUR FINGERS, SOFT AS THE SUN
    MOLD YOUR FISTS, BIG AS YOUR HEART
    TRACE YOUR ARMS, TILL NIGHT TURNS TO MORNING
    DON'T NEED THE STARS,
    LET ME BE PART OF YOUR BODY

KAHEKILI. Den she kiss me on da fron' a da head,
    turn my body into one star, li'dat everyt'ing jus' hard
    rock hard.

    An' befo' I can say stop I'm da star and she not,

    she fall an' fall an' fall toward da watah,

    but I can hear her she call out fo' me,

    she go she go,

GUIDEBOOK. "Bye baby,
    I'm not sad you never knew me
    I'll find you in Maui."

    The best and only way to get to Maui is air travel.
    Although Hawaii's islands lie in close proximity to each
    other, the currents of the Pacific run so deep and wild
    through the channels, that not even the bravest of sea
    warriors could brave the waves.

But while you're up there, be sure to peer down at the great island of paradise. The shape of Maui has been likened to that of a snowman, lying diagonally towards west, embracing all weary travelers from near and far.

JESSIEE. Hate planes. Hate, hate, hate planes.

I'm sitting in 25A, squashed up between a view of the Pacific sea, and this very huge marine and his tales of nine different spinal surgeries. Two hours in and he's about to show me a scar that –

GUIDEBOOK. "Runs from my ear to the shoulder blade, blade to the T12, T12 to bladder, then to the tailbone. Kinda looks like a dragon. A skinny dragon."

JESSIEE. So I pretend to fall asleep. Which he takes as a cue to fall asleep too. On my shoulder.

I'm thirty-two – too old for this to be cute, you know?

But I'm stuck here, barely breathing for the fear of cracking yet another thoracic something in this poor man's body.

And I could just hear my mom,

GUIDEBOOK. "Ha, think you can leave me here and be free, that's where you end up, wedged in there like a thumb in an asshole."

JESSIEE. No, that's unfair. She'd never say that. In fact, she's barely said anything in the past couple months.

She's depressed.

She's –

But no more sad things.

My mom, bless her soul, is the most angelic, beautiful, clueless person in the world,

faithful to the church, faithful to the world, faithful to her faith.

She got cancer somewhere in the knees, had to get them both chopped off, the cancer and the knees – not that it helped –

Still thinks the worst thing about being legless is that she can't kneel down to pray.

So when I announced that I'm, headed for the hulas and Mai Tais of the west sun, all she said was,

GUIDEBOOK. "Be safe, okay?"

JESSIEE. I said I'd bring back a grandchild for her, would she mind boy or girl or something in between.

She said,

GUIDEBOOK. "Oh, oh, how about those, macadamia nut things covered with chocolate?

Those are Hawaiian, aren't they?"

JESSIEE. I'm thinking serves me right, abandoning your legless mom to go catch a frog, I'm thinking, yeh, this right here is the rest of the trip, my smallness wedged between the world's rude largeness, no way I'll ever budge from my small stupid seat.

And then I start to feel funny, count the dates and realize, yay, menstruating.

To my right, dreaming marine, to my left, the Pacific.

What to do?

Stay put and soon we'd both be sitting in a pool of blood – day one, I go pretty anemic – Climb out from my gorge, and I might break him or wake him,

and well

he looked so peaceful.

So what's a girl to do?

This is what I do.

Find a tampon, slide hand into pants – all of which are expertly concealed by coat and blanket.

Then slowly, silently, with the focus of Mister Miyagi,

pop the sucker in.

Yup, all this in the confines of 25A, y'all.

The audacity of taking care of personal needs in public spaces. That's accomplishment, people.

And I was like, yeh. I can do this, I'm going to Maui.

KAHEKILI. Love planes. Love, love, love planes.

Bruh, what miracle, y'know, flyin'.

Monster engine growl down da road, den wind an' air
tek over, li'dat, tek over,
lift up dis whole mansion a people up, up, up, an'
whooooooooshshhhhmmm.

Was one trip wid my fadda, y'know, dis plane ride.
Dis boy, ten years old, fadda an' son, we's goin' pipeline.
Billabong Pipeline Masters,
dass one odda Triple Crown of Surfing, y'know.
Shoots, bruh, dis my fadda's time, any one back home
dey know, Haw, he can ride any kine wave, dis kine dat
kine all da kines,
he be taking one odda t'ree triple crowns, fo' sure
Nanahnanahnanahnanah!

He neva got it.

We neva even got deh. Pipeline beach? Nah.
He took wid us his woman, yah? Dey fight every minute
an' second,
an' li'dat all *huhu* she leaves us da night befo' da fuckin'
day of the tournament,
an' he go drunk walk all over Waikiki till
some tourist wen run over his big toe.

You wanna kill da rising surfer, plenny easy.
Jus' buss up da buggah's big toe.

Fadda neva say any kine t'ing about dat accident.
Neva say any kine t'ing about anyt'ing no more,
jus' sit deh carving tiny *honu* from scraps a wood, eh,
honu keyring, *honu* magnet *honu* whatevadafuck, fucking
ugly little buggahs.
Sell 'em on da beach fo' da *haoles*, da kine tourist.

Dat plane back home.
Dat be my second an' last plane ride.
To my right, tiny window.
To my left, tiny man.
My shrinking fadda wid da drinks, wid da cryin'.

Dis boy, dis ten-year-old boy doing any t'ing he can to not stare at dis fadda's buss up toe,

to not stare at dis hero giant, da kine, neh.

An' I remember t'inking, Today one life wen pau. Dis buss up toe, it wen *pau* one life.

Dat life not my life.

My life neva gon' drink one drink,

neva gon' go *lolo* ova li'dat, a woman.

No need fly anyweh other place, No need no odda person,

Me I'm gon' keep all a my toes stayin' right here, in my island, Maui.

(In-flight seat belt release "ping.")

GUIDEBOOK. Aloha and welcome to Maui, Hawaii, one of the most desired destinations on the planet. With over two and half million visitors almost every year, we know that you know that Maui is the most happiest place to be.

KAHEKILI. Marry me.

*(Ukulele.)***

JESSIEE. We should tell the stories in order.

KAHEKILI. Marry me.

(Ukulele.)

JESSIEE. People will be confused.

KAHEKILI. Marry me! Jessiee with two ees. Marry me.

(Ukulele.)

(Ukulele.)

JESSIEE. So he asks me,

out of the blue to marry him.

I've known this guy for what, barely a week, so I say…

[This isn't working.]

These moments should be treated as **GUIDEBOOK's non-verbal lines.

This isn't working. Start at the beginning.

(Ukulele.)

I said, back it up!

GUIDEBOOK. With over two and half million visitors almost every year, we know that you know that Maui is the most happiest place to be.

(In-flight seat belt release "ping.")

(As flight captain.) Aloha and welcome to Maui, the current temperature is 79 degrees,

local time is Friday, January 26, 2:52 a.m. Thank you for flying with us this morning, we hope you enjoy your stay. *Mahalo.*

JESSIEE. With a thud, the plane lands,

I bid good luck to Mister Marine, watch him hug the life out of some sleepy happy girl.

The whole airport smells of sleepy happy people. I'm a bit lost. I've never done this before you know, travel for pleasure. I consult the guidebook and he says,

GUIDEBOOK.

KA'ANAPALI

KA'ANAPALI

PRETTY PARADISE AT SEA

KA'ANAPALI

KAHEKILI. Ka'anapali Beach.

Usually not good for mornings, too small an' lappish da surf stay yeh?

We watahmen call dose tourist waves, good for pictures good for paddling good for not'ing.

But today, I t'ink,

GUIDEBOOK.

KA'ANAPALI

KAHEKILI. I wek up look up at da sky an' t'ink,

GUIDEBOOK.

KA'ANAPALI

JESSIEE. So I think okay, why not.

GUIDEBOOK.

WHERE THE WAVES ARE YOUNG AND FREE
KA'ANAPALI

(*As rental car receptionist.*) Yeah, man, we're all out of the open cars, they go pretty fast, you know? All we got is a couple compacts and a whole lotta SUVs. Do you want insurance with that?

> (**JESSIEE**'s *phone rings.*)
>
> (*She ignores it.*)

(*As rental car receptionist.*) Blue Hyundai straight down, somewhere on your left. Have fun, man, *mahalo.*

GRAB A BOARD AND RIDE THE PASSING TIDE
GRAB A SNORKEL LET THE WORRIES SLIDE
EVERYTHING'S EASY, IN KA'ANAPALI
WHEN THE CORAL REEFS COME OUT TO PLAY
OCEAN WONDERS BRIGHTEN UP THE BAY
OF KA'ANAPALI,

JESSIEE & KAHEKILI. Ka'anapali.

KAHEKILI. Strange how quiet it stay dis day.

Even early morning y'know, eh, people laughin', gettin' drunk somewhere. Ka'anapali stay separate planet on Maui – Planet Tourist.

But dis day not one buggah, not one sound.

JESSIEE. The whole place is lit by the stars. I've never seen anything lit by the stars before.

KAHEKILI. Den deh by da shore I see da lady y'know, from my dream,

> (**JESSIEE**'s *phone rings.*)

And I thought, lady has phone, kay, not my dream.

> (*A loud splash, a body thrown into a mass of water. No more phone.*)

First t'ought, fucking tourists fucking stop chucking shit into my *'aina* –

Second t'ought, lady jus' t'row her phone in da sea. Normal people don't do dat.

GUIDEBOOK. Off of the point, there are strong currents at times, so use caution.

(JESSIEE *sits on the beach.*)

(KAHEKILI *comes up to her.*)

KAHEKILI. *Aloha,* howzit, eh?

JESSIEE. My god, you scared me!

KAHEKILI. Haw, sorry, jus', everyt'ing good? You good, eh?

JESSIEE. Excuse me?

KAHEKILI. You t'rew your phone into da watah.

JESSIEE. Oh. Yes. I did.

KAHEKILI. Y'know I don't know how come you do dat but you shouldn't do dat. Maybe you wen hit swimming *honu* on his head an' den his 300-year-old life *pau.*

JESSIEE. Excuse me?

KAHEKILI. Have to stay respectful odda ocean, y'know.

JESSIEE. Sorry. You're probably thinking, stupid tourists,

KAHEKILI. Fo' sure, but you t'inking, stupid locals, so we even, neh?

(JESSIEE *smiles.*)

KAHEKILI. So how come you do dat?

JESSIEE. Do what? Oh, phone. I'm, getting off the grid. You know, Maui, no worries, free as a bird,

KAHEKILI. Maui is off da grid, yah?

JESSIEE. If you're from Akron, Ohio, yeah.

KAHEKILI. Kay den, how come you getting off da grid?

JESSIEE. Funny story actually – Do you want the bullshit version or the real one.

KAHEKILI. Da funny one.

JESSIEE. Maybe it's not that funny. I'm visiting, taking a well-deserved break from my busy important life.

KAHEKILI. Yah, dass not dat funny.

JESSIEE. Actually I'm an escaped convict running from the international police with my bag full of cash and high-grade dope.

KAHEKILI. Haw.

JESSIEE. Yup.

KAHEKILI. Fo' real?

JESSIEE. Yeah, for real. Wanna look? Look.

> (**JESSIEE** *holds out her bag.*)

> (**KAHEKILI** *takes a look, tentative.*)

Ohmygod you totally / fell for that!

KAHEKILI. Yah yah well you gon' say sumt'ing about money and dope most Hawaiian boys gon' wan' look.

JESSIEE. Sorry to disappoint I'm just a little ol' girl with her boring little knapsack looking for her long-lost chance at happiness.

KAHEKILI. Ah, you one a dose.

JESSIEE. One of what?

KAHEKILI. Plenny mainland people come Maui fo' find "happiness."

JESSIEE. Glad to be clumped in with the general public.

KAHEKILI. You angry! I apologize, I only say you come da right place.

JESSIEE. Not angry at all. I'm generally clumped in with the general public. I spring from the heart of that general indistinguishable lump of boring, small and predictable.

KAHEKILI. I only meant you have come to da right place.

JESSIEE. Thanks, I guess.

> …

I don't normally do this.

KAHEKILI. ?

JESSIEE. This, with you, I don't like talking to strangers,

KAHEKILI. "My name is Kahekili Ke'aloha. Nice to meet you." Now we good.

JESSIEE. Totally. All better.

KAHEKILI. "And what is your name, miss?"

JESSIEE. Nicole.

KAHEKILI. Nicole…

JESSIEE. Kidman.

KAHEKILI. Like da movie actress, neh?

JESSIEE. It's a joke.

KAHEKILI. You a funny lady.

JESSIEE. Not really.

KAHEKILI. Kay den, "Ms. Kidman, the surfs are most beautiful today. Might I interest you to be scuba diving for happiness?"

JESSIEE. *(To audience.)* He's quick funny and hot as a nugget. I see his hands roughed up by waves and sands I imagine,

his dark black hair, wetted to his tanned forehead, glimmering on a sunny…

I am very much sexing out on this stranger surfer man.

KAHEKILI. Y'know, Ka'anapali Beach is da most popular beach for safe scuba diving.

JESSIEE. You know how exotic vacation spots do that to you. It's like a little travel package: tiny toiletries, large libido.

KAHEKILI. Or maybe surfing? Great breaks today for first time surfers.

JESSIEE. He keeps talking and talking and I keep dreaming the wrong…

KAHEKILI. You not know happiness till you wen meet dis *'aina*'s rippling waves, li'dat.

JESSIEE. And I'm like, Ripple me home honey.

KAHEKILI. We go neh?

JESSIEE. Uh, I'll think about you, it.

KAHEKILI. Dass one no, I know, when lady say, I'll t'ink about it, it means take a walk, fella.

JESSIEE. Yup, that's a no.

KAHEKILI. How come?

JESSIEE. Can't swim.

KAHEKILI. Wha!

JESSIEE. What.

KAHEKILI. I don't know what dat's like. Can't swim.

JESSIEE. It's not a disability or anything I just don't do it,

KAHEKILI. I teach you, eh? All da time I do dis.

JESSIEE. Do what, seduce unassuming ladies into waddling into the water with you and then have your way with them?

Coz I'm not against that.

KAHEKILI. I just meant swimming, eh, but if you go li'dat, y'know. I'm not against.

JESSIEE. If you're not and I'm not,

…why are we…not?

And I'm thinking, where did that come from?

KAHEKILI. You a funny lady.

JESSIEE. Funny ladies are softer on the inside. Wanna find out?

Seriously, who's this woman talking?

KAHEKILI. She mek me laugh, like a long time ago.

JESSIEE. And maybe the sand on my bare feet is just foreign enough.

KAHEKILI. And maybe da breaks odda beach, rhythm enough.

JESSIEE. Maybe his fingers, familiar enough.

KAHEKILI. Maybe her laugh, sad enough.

(They kiss long enough, sweet enough.)

JESSIEE. Read somewhere, we keep our trauma locked up in our muscles,

KAHEKILI. Someone say, we keep our stories hidden in da body,

can not shake it off,

can not let it go,

JESSIEE. And sometimes,

we find someone that finds them. Our hidden stories.

(They think.)

(They do it again, longer, warmer.)

(GUIDEBOOK gently begins to underscore this moment with the previously introduced Hawaiian song, allowing space for the characters to swell.)

(He continues to sing as KAHEKILI and JESSIEE begin to speak, and the words, the movement, and the music weave into a beautiful dance.)

KAHEKILI. I'm on plane, flying again,
    Monster engine between my thighs,

JESSIEE. Like the ocean,
    He moved like the ocean.

KAHEKILI. Whooooooooshshshmmmm.
    An' den we lift up, up, up.

JESSIEE. And I'm thinking
    "What are you doing, Jessiee.
    Step on the brakes, Jessiee.
    Also, if you're gonna do this, chuck your tampon Jessiee.

KAHEKILI. Wha?

    (Music stops abruptly.)

JESSIEE. Hmm?

KAHEKILI. You t'rew somet'ing over,

JESSIEE. What?

KAHEKILI. I t'ink I saw – You t'rew something into da sea.

JESSIEE. Glass, pebble, thing, it was, you know, my back, something hurting my back,
    or tampon, it was my tampon, I threw my tampon into your sea.

KAHEKILI. Haw.

JESSIEE. It is biodegradable.

KAHEKILI. Wha?

JESSIEE. Dissolves. Into fish food.

KAHEKILI. Haw.

JESSIEE. Should I go get it back?

KAHEKILI. Nah.

JESSIEE. That's worse, right?

KAHEKILI. Yah.

> **(GUIDEBOOK** *expertly intervenes, picking up where we left off before the tampon interruption.)*
>
> *(When the song comes to the end of a verse.)*

JESSIEE. Our clothes lay on the shore,

KAHEKILI. Our bodies wrapped widda sand,

JESSIEE. The stars were unbelievably, many.

> *(Music ends in a question.)*

And then something strange happens, maybe he did hit a memory nerve. Somewhere between his ribs and my belly, a slide of his palm and I am back fifteen years, high school, with a voice of a boy I'd long locked away.

BOY. *(Played by* **GUIDEBOOK.***)* So that one's Ursa Major, you know the Big Dipper, right?

And that's her son, Ursa Minor. Ursa is Latin for bear.

JESSIEE. A boy obsessed with constellations, poking holes into his milk box sky for the science fair.

BOY. These four outline the body, the ladle part is the tail.

JESSIEE. He was going through all of the holes he had poked, going through all of the stories behind those holes. Love of my life, today his best friend was the toothpick.

BOY. Then one day, the boy hunter was roaming the woods, as was the lady bear.

In one sad fated moment, the two locked eyes,

Callisto in bear form, rushed towards the boy hunter,

to give him a hug, or to beat the shit out of him, I don't know, but the boy hunter thought the latter,

coz he / got out his bow and arrow, swift as lightning, drew the sinew,

JESSIEE. Got out his bow and arrow, swift as lightning, drew the sinew,

BOY. And just before something really sad happened, / a divine intervention!

JESSIEE. A divine intervention.

Story goes, Zeus, who'd originally knocked up Callisto, felt bad and so mother and son were whirled up to the constellations as mom bear and baby bear.

They are now happy, and playing together,

but who knows.

Maybe they're frozen in combat, still unclear as to who they are to each other.

BOY. You see, over there, that's the mom's head, that's baby's foot.

JESSIEE. I'm pretty sure the mom bear was running to hug her child, not to trash him.

BOY. How would you know?

JESSIEE. I know, I'm a girl, I have maternal instincts.

Now it's time to go to my mom's bedroom and have sex.

BOY. Is that a maternal instinct too?

JESSIEE. Maybe.

Come on, Benji, my mom will be back in like an hour.

BOY. We should have our own star story. What would it be?

JESSIEE. Come on, Benji. Benji. Hoi Ben. Benjamin. Benjamino.

Boink.

BOY. Boink back.

JESSIEE. Double boink.

BOY. Jessie stop it I'm trying to concentrate.

JESSIEE. Benji… [let's go to Mom and Dad's bedroom and have sex.]

BOY. Again? It's like all you ever want to do now. Jessie I love you but sometimes I'm sorry we discovered sex.

KAHEKILI. Cold? You got like chicken skin. We go fo' swim in da watah, neh, in da watah, warm da bodies stay.

JESSIEE. I don't usually swim.

KAHEKILI. I t'ink today da day fo' doing t'ings you not usually do.

JESSIEE. No.

KAHEKILI. You good? You lookin' da kine.

JESSIEE. Da what?

KAHEKILI. Like you look at me but you not see me.

JESSIEE. Yeh, Sorry, I just, no I'm fine. I don't like large masses of water, it freaks me out. How it, um, how it keeps moving all the time, oh my god all this sand, I am covered in sand.

KAHEKILI. Da beach, lotta sand, y'know, how it is.

JESSIEE. I'm, sand. Too much sand.

Drink. I think a drink! Is it too early or too late? It's Maui, I'm sure something will be open.

KAHEKILI. Nah. I neva drink.

JESSIEE. Eh? I don't swim, you don't drink, clearly we're not meant to be together.

Come on, it's a special night. Just one drink. Where's the night scene happenin' in this town –

KAHEKILI. Haw, slow slow, Miss Nicole. Da sun be up soon, no bar open anywhere on dis island.

An' even if deh be, I couldn't get in.

JESSIEE. You blacklisted or something?

KAHEKILI. What, no! Under-aged.

JESSIEE. Huh.

KAHEKILI. What.

JESSIEE. How under-aged.

KAHEKILI. Fifteen.

JESSIEE. Huh.

KAHEKILI. What?

JESSIEE. Of course.

KAHEKILI. Nicole. What, li'dat, haw wait Nicole.

JESSIEE. Don't wait Nicole me, you're fifteen. I've just committed a crime. I mean, unless Maui years are like dog years to Ohio years.

KAHEKILI. Wha? Nicole, wait, for real, you go you go? Nicole!

JESSIEE. My name is not Nicole! Also, stop talking to me!

KAHEKILI. For real?

JESSIEE. For real what.

KAHEKILI. For real stop? Dass it? One number change everyt'ing you see?

JESSIEE. You are fifteen. That is a big number for me, okay?

KAHEKILI. Her problem my age, y'know?
Dass like, I can't jus' tek back, say,
actually no, I'm sixteen, or some odda number dat mek you feel better.
So I jus' say,
Kay den. What is your name, Nicole. Real name.

JESSIEE. Jessiee. With two ees.

KAHEKILI. You have good time in Maui, kay, Jessiee with two ees? Aloha.
I'm t'inking, no need, y'know? I'm a man a da watah, no need fo' no woman li'dat, yah?

JESSIEE. And he just stands up, dusts off his butt and starts to leave.

KAHEKILI. I come fo' ride da breaks, no need some crazy *haole* lady who look for "happiness."

JESSIEE. I'm sitting there like what just happened, but also don't go don't go, don't go pretty man with pretty hands after all what is a number it's just a number, no the number is fifteen you do not get to perv out on fifteen –

KAHEKILI. But befo' I know what when how,

JESSIEE. Suddenly he turns, walks back to me,

KAHEKILI. My mout' opens and say,
I dive fo' Black Rock ritual tonight. Come. Tek pictures.
An' den buy me my drink, neh?
An' I'm like,
Haw. Not bad brah.
An' befo' she say no or yes, I turn around and shoot straight da odda way.

JESSIEE. I watch his silhouette shrink into a dot
His unbelievably hot, stop it, fifteen-year-old dot.

I put my shirt back on, switch the crazy off and decide, sleep.

GUIDEBOOK. Be sure to secure accommodations before you arrive! For the full treatment, Maui resorts can't be beat when visiting Hawaii. Living in ultimate island luxury may keep you from ever leaving the property, until the bill comes.

(As hotel front desk.) I'm sorry ma'am. The only vacancy at this time is our deluxe Oceanfront suite available to you at the Endless Escape Rate of $519 a night. How long are you planning to stay with us?

(JESSIEE gives him a credit card.)

JESSIEE. I still feel this boy all over.

I still feel his hands all over.

Tanned, rough on the outside soft on the inside,

And I'm like, stop it Jessiee, stop re-feeling the teenager's hands, his slowly pulsing, grating but not too much, rough-ish smooth-ish,

GUIDEBOOK. *(As hotel front desk.)* I am very sorry ma'am but it seems your card is not going through?

(JESSIEE gives him another credit card.)

JESSIEE. Fingers! His hands had fingers.

Boys back home, no fingers, it's like grope grope, smoosh and squish, but oh fingers. Touching, lingering, not just passing through to get to home base, fingers...

GUIDEBOOK. *(As hotel front desk.)* I apologize ma'am but,

(JESSIEE gives him another credit card.)

JESSIEE. I have an obsession with hands. Like, obsession. If I could I would build a shrine of hands.

GUIDEBOOK. *(As hotel front desk.)* Excellent. Your bill will be available upon checkout. Complimentary breakfast is served in our open air Black Rock Terrace at seven a.m., elevators to your left. Have a wonderful stay.

JESSIEE. Just, tells you so much about a person.

Is this a hand that's known more dishwater or office paper. Have these fingers spent more time curled into fists or sifting through someone's hair. Is this a grip that will clutch at your heart or at your throat. Or both. Or neither.

Just by touch you know. You know?

BOY. I think it's a little pervie.

I mean yeh hands are great and they let you do stuff, but you? You get all focused and intense when you talk about hands, and I'm telling you it gets a little pervie sometimes. It's like sometimes I think, is Jessiee gonna creep up on me one night chop off my hands and run away with them, coz actually that's all she wants from me?

(**JESSIEE** *looks at the* **BOY,** *who has maybe laid his head on her lap.*)

JESSIEE. His hands were a little different, though.

A tender pair of hands,

a pair that hadn't gone through enough of its life to have worn much of its owner's stories.

I can't imagine what those hands might look like today, how they might casually rest on the driver's steering wheel, finger a cigarette or two, sooth their master's chin with a cool aftershave.

BOY. My hands are real big for a ninth grader.

I should take up something, guitar or basketball, something where big hands are appreciated.

JESSIEE. I appreciate them.

BOY. Just when they do stuff for you.

(**BOY**'s *hands start to do stuff for* **JESSIEE***…*)

KAHEKILI. Haw, bruh, I get home t'row my board up against da wall an' tek some ice for dis my *ule.*

Li'dat my little man, I wen rub him up against some serious grains a sand nuh, buggah be purple!

UGH!

Shoots, bruh, da ocean, she always ready wid some new kine da painful stuff.

But I love dis.

My purple penis, neh?

Da hurt mek you into somet'ing else nah?

Y'scrap some, y'bleed some,

an' da blood from da scrap, get you goin', get you harder, get you stronger, till you know you strong enough fo' tek off da shirt an' scrap wid da big bruddas out deh.

NAH? NAH? Ha.

Yeh, deh I stay wid dis pack a frozen broccoli rollin' over my *ule*, my fadda come home wid a new pile a scrap wood and da stink a death on his face.

We don't even talk now, not even.

Li'dat, he see his dinner on his boy's balls an' he just pass on by, li'dat.

Jus' li'dat.

Pass on by.

Shoots brah, like I wanna talk with him, neh?

Nah. Forget about it.

(*JESSIEE stops* **BOY**.)

JESSIEE. What happened to the science project?

BOY. Which one?

JESSIEE. You were building a sky with milk cartons and a toothpick, with those fighting bears –

BOY. Oh yeh, switched up for lemon lamplight.

Don't you remember, I smelled like lemons for two weeks. Why?

JESSIEE. Just wondering.

BOY. Makes me nervous when you start wondering things, Jessie. You never just wonder things.

JESSIEE. I don't?

BOY. Nope. What's up.

JESSIEE. No. Nothing. Forget about it.

(**BOY** *shrugs, continues what he was doing.*)

KAHEKILI. Jus' li'dat.

Pass on by.

But y'know, what would I say, if he ass about my *ule*.

Fadda man, I wen stick dis little man in one *haole* lady at da beach, Jessiee, wid two ees, wid her boring bag an' her biode-chamacallit blood sponge t'ing, an' your boy don't know how fo' stop t'inking about dis lady,

an' I don't know maybe she be my wife she be my family. What you t'ink about dat, eh?

Yeh Fadda man anodda t'ing I got that you don't got.

Li'dat, Fadda you make me sick how not'ing you are, like I wanna say dat?

I'd chop off all ten a my toes to get myself anodda fadda who taller den me,

like I wanna say dat?

Shoots brah, like I wanna say dat?

He not hard enough to hear dat.

(**JESSIEE** *stops* **BOY** *again.*)

JESSIEE. It's not fair.

BOY. What now?

JESSIEE. It wasn't their fault, either of them.

BOY. Whose fault? What?

JESSIEE. The bears.

BOY. Bears.

JESSIEE. It wasn't their fault, they didn't know enough, they had the right to try and protect themselves, you know? People have the right to draw an arrow on a bear running towards them or to whup the shit out of a hunter trying to kill them,

people have a right to protect themselves from harm.

It's not okay that we're all glad that this big cosmic dick came and intervened, whipped them up into balls of gas in the sky not even as people, but as bears,

and that's the good part, it's just not fair.

BOY. Jessie. Tell me what's wrong.

JESSIEE. Everything.

BOY. Just pick one and tell me.

JESSIEE. I'm pregnant.

But, no more sad things.

Maui! Beach Sex! Clean bed! I check in, close the blinds, take a pill and check the fuck out!

> (**BOY** *is a* **GUIDEBOOK**, *and* **GUIDEBOOK** *drums, drums furiously and wistfully on something. In Polynesian rhythms.*)

GUIDEBOOK. The Legend of Lele Kawa on Black Rock Cliff. Legend tells us the last chief of Maui, Kahekili proved his spiritual strength by leaping from sacred Pu'u Keka'a to the Pacific.

> (*Boom. Drum.*)

KAHEKILI & JESSIEE. I wake with a start,

JESSIEE. Where the hell am I?

KAHEKILI. I musta wen tek one nap,

JESSIEE. Can't tell if it's day or night,

KAHEKILI. Don't know if dat sun be coming or going?

GUIDEBOOK. As the sun begins his slow dive into the ocean, torch lighting signals the start of a nightly ritual of Lele Kawa on Black Rock Cliff.

JESSIEE. I've slept through the day,

KAHEKILI. I am late,

JESSIEE. Am I late? Did I miss him?

> (*Drums beat on, perhaps the diver is a shadow puppet climbing a shadow Black Rock.*)

GUIDEBOOK. (*As ceremony emcee at hotel.*) With sunset painting the sky, a young cliff diver honors his heritage by re-tracing footsteps in the sand on Ka'anapali Beach.

JESSIEE. Sorry, hi, where's the diving thing happening?

GUIDEBOOK. *(As emcee.)* A chant of old Hawai'i begins the progression of our warrior;

JESSIEE. Hello, excuse me, I'm looking for Black Rock? Some kind of diving?

GUIDEBOOK. *(As emcee.)* The echo of the conch shell announces his arrival.

    (Conch shell blows.)

JESSIEE. There he was.

GUIDEBOOK. *(As emcee.)* He leaves a trail of glowing torches surrounding the lagoon as he makes his way to Black Rock.

JESSIEE. Tiny man atop the cliff, like the tiny frog on my index finger,

GUIDEBOOK. *(As emcee.)* Upon reaching the summit, he offers his flaming torch to the ocean below,

JESSIEE. There he was.

GUIDEBOOK. *(As emcee.)* Casts his flower *lei* into the sea;

JESSIEE. At the edge of the cliff.

GUIDEBOOK. *(As emcee.)* And finally takes the breathtaking dive,

JESSIEE. Staring out into the –

GUIDEBOOK. *(As emcee.)* From Black Rock into the rolling surf below.

JESSIEE. No!

    (Drum. Boom.)

    (The shadow diver leaps off the Rock.)

BOY. We should name him Benjamin after me.

JESSIEE. We could also name him Jessie after me.

BOY. Jessie is a girl name.

JESSIEE. It can be a boy name.

    Also we don't know Jessie is a boy. Could be a girl.

BOY. Oh, if he's a girl then we should name her Jasmin. Half of your name, half of mine.

JESSIEE. Jasmin's a Disney princess.

BOY. Okay, then Bessie, half of my name, half of –

JESSIEE. Bessie's a cow.

BOY. Hey. Why you so cranky?

JESSIEE. I'm not. I just, can't believe we're gonna do this. It's crazy.

BOY. No it's not. People had babies in their teens all the time.

JESSIEE. Those people didn't have to take SATs.

BOY. You still wanna do that, huh?

JESSIEE. Maybe.

BOY. We'll figure it out. My mom will help, we could get a tutor or something, you could live with us,

JESSIEE. You told her?!

BOY. 'Course not.
    Not yet. We're gonna have to, at some point.

JESSIEE. She's gonna make us get rid of it.
    I know my mom will.

BOY. We could run away? We could run away some place far, like Robinson Crusoe, to an island,

JESSIEE. Robinson Crusoe was shipwrecked, Benji.

BOY. Then – I mean, whatever, we can still go to an island. We could go to Hawaii. I could catch things in the sea, teach Jasmin how to hula,

JESSIEE. You know how to hula?

BOY. I could learn while she is growing up.

JESSIEE. Girl hula and boy hula is different.

BOY. I'll learn how to girl hula. For Jasmin. And also boy hula, if it's a Benjamin.

JESSIEE. All of this is a really horrible plan.

BOY. You have no romantic notions.

JESSIEE. I have a thing growing in me yes I have no romantic notions.
    I have a thing growing in me.

It's been growing.

Benjamin.

It's gonna keep growing.

BOY. I know.

JESSIEE. It's been over two months, I don't think they can even –

BOY. Well we're not doing that.

JESSIEE. Well we're not going to Hawaii.

BOY. You're so serious. It's like I don't even know you any more. Jess I love you but sometimes I'm sorry we discovered sex.

JESSIEE. Ben I love you but sometimes I wish you'd fucking grow up.

> (*A loud splash, a body thrown into a mass of water.*)

GUIDEBOOK. Be sure to enjoy this nightly tradition at the poolside Cliff Dive Bar at Sheraton Maui.

> (**JESSIEE** *waits.*)

JESSIEE. He does this for a living, there's no way anything would happen,

even if it did what do I care, I just met him,

barely met him barely a one night stand, illegal one night stand, I shouldn't even be here,

but I sit here, I keep scanning the horizon, squinting, searching for a head bobbing up and down,

still no head,

Do you do that?

That thing where you have images of, blades slashing your hands when you blend a smoothie, buses smashing into your ribs when you step off the sidewalk, volcanic rocks splitting into your head when you jump off a cliff.

Still no head.

I'm thinking nothing's wrong, calm the fuck down.

But you know, it's like reflex a self-defense thing,

where when something bad might happen,

even if that "might" is a miniscule little fraction of a possibility, your mind jumps to that image, savors that image, lets that image be, in your head,

so when you find out that your mom's legs will be chopped off you could be like oh phew,

I thought she was gonna die a slow and smelly death while she bankrupts the entire world, wheelchair? Sure I can deal with that.

I can deal with a lot of things, just gotta make it seem not as bad as the really bad thing.

But if the thought of the really bad thing – even when it's not real, not real at all, still makes you feel icky and vomitty and just green in the face almost as bad as if it were real, then what's the point, is there a point, still no head! Where's the head?

Did he float up a corpse and nobody can see coz it's so dark? How'd it get so dark, so soon, the sun Just set!

I should call the police,

maybe I'm the only one who was really watching,

maybe he's a gun for hire, light the torch, jump the cliff, job well done and nobody cares,

maybe I'm his only hope for a decent burial before he's ripped up into shark / food –

KAHEKILI. Hi.

JESSIEE. Aaaaaaaaaaaaaaaaaaaaaaaaaaaaaaaaaaaaaaaarrrrrrrrgh!

KAHEKILI. …

JESSIEE. How did you get here.

KAHEKILI. I – You okay?

JESSIEE. There was no head.

KAHEKILI. There was no head…?

JESSIEE. I was watching this whole time. For your head. You never came up. How'd you, I didn't even see, My God don't you ever do that again.

KAHEKILI. I swim around da rock fo' get back.

Ritual, ceremony, everyt'ing very beautiful, y'know, nobody gon' wanna see da help. Kill da magic.

I am sorry fo' mek you worry.

—

It is nice, t'ough. Dat I mek someone worry.

(A moment.)

(Phone rings.)

GUIDEBOOK. *(As hotel bellboy.)* Sorry to interrupt, ma'am, but you have a call waiting at the front desk.

(No.)

JESSIEE. And then a week went by. Learnt things about Maui. Things people generally learn about new places in a week,

GUIDEBOOK.

DRIVE ALONG THE ROAD TO SANCTUARY
WATCH THE WATERS FALL IN HARMONY
NATURE'S KAHUNA THE ROAD TO HANA,

KAHEKILI. Chiiiiiiiiiiiiiiiiiiiii-ho!

JESSIEE. Chiiiiiiiiiiiiiiiiiiiiii-ho! Faster! Faster! Faster!

KAHEKILI. Dis plenny fast, Jessiee.

JESSIEE. Aw is baby scared? Does baby want me to drive?

KAHEKILI. It's li'dat, huh? Kay den Jessiee wid two ees, you about to t'row up all kine stuff –

Ae Ae Ae / Chiiiiiiiiiiiiiiiiiiiiii-ho!

JESSIEE. Chiiiiiiiiiiiiiiiiiiiiii-ho!

GUIDEBOOK.

GOTTA TAKE YOUR TIME WITH TURNS AND TRIALS,
WITH 54 BRIDGES AND 600 CURVES IN 50 MILES
OH YOU DON'T WANNA SPEED DOWN TO HANA –

(JESSIEE throws up.)

KAHEKILI. Shoots, you good? Jessiee.

JESSIEE. No worries I'm totally – [fine.]

(JESSIEE tries to not throw up.)

KAHEKILI. Here, tek some coconut watah, yah? Mek you feel –

> (**JESSIEE** *throws up on him.*)

GUIDEBOOK.

> FIND A SPOT TO READ WHILE GETTING TANNED
> FIND THE SHORE OF SOFTEST WHITEST SAND
> COME TO NAPILI, FINEST IN MAUI

KAHEKILI. You come beach, you go watah. I don't understand dis come beach fo' read book, Jessiee.

JESSIEE. It's what grown-ups like to do. You'll understand when you are older.

> (**KAHEKILI** *takes book, reads.*)

KAHEKILI. "…He sucks each of my nipples hard, then follows the line of ice cream down my –" Ice cream?

JESSIEE. For some people.

> (*Awkward.*)

Oh my god, what the hell is that. Is that a sea lion, I think it's a sea lion!

GUIDEBOOK.

> A MONK SEAL MIGHT FIND HIS WAY TO SHORE
> SOAKING IN THE ADORATION FOR

> (*Monk seal singing sounds "Arp arp arp."*)

> WILDLIFE OF MAUI

JESSIEE. Oooh helllooo purty purty.

KAHEKILI. No, no touch!

JESSIEE. Why? Does it bite?

KAHEKILI. It is illegal.

JESSIEE. You're illegal. Come on, can I at least take a picture with him?

KAHEKILI. Haw, tourists.

JESSIEE. Don't be such a local. Embrace the touristy! The world is so beautiful!

GUIDEBOOK.

> VOLCANIC MOUNTAINS RISE UP TO THE SKIES

FROZEN LAVA HUMS THE LULLABIES
DON'T MISS THE SUNRISE AT HALEAKALA,

JESSIEE. It's five fucking a.m.

KAHEKILI. You tole me you want fo' see da sunrise.

JESSIEE. Out my hotel window, in bed sipping coffee.

KAHEKILI. You stay such da tourist, you must embrace da local.

GUIDEBOOK.

WEATHER CAN BE UNPREDICTABLE
10,000 FEET ABOVE SEA LEVEL...

JESSIEE. I can't feel my face I can't feel my face.

KAHEKILI. Say cheese,

JESSIEE. You say cheese I can't fucking feel my fucking face.

KAHEKILI. *Hele mai.* Come fo' me.

> *(Hugs her into his windbreaker.)*
>
> *(She burrows her face into his chest.)*
>
> *(JESSIEE inaudibly rants displeasure and general early morning crankiness from his chest.)*

KAHEKILI. Eh, look.

> *(JESSIEE peaks out from his jacket.)*
>
> *(The sun is rising over the clouds.)*

JESSIEE. Oh –

Wow.

> *(They take it in.)*

KAHEKILI. *Hale'akala,* House of da Sun.

> *(They look on for a good while.)*
>
> *(They really want to kiss.)*
>
> *(A phone rings.)*

GUIDEBOOK. *(As hotel bellboy.)* Sorry to interrupt but there's a call awaiting you at the front desk, ma'am.

> *(No.)*

JESSIEE. There was a lot of no sex happening.

My little travel package was like, "Oh come oooooooon, seriously? We're in Maui it is Mutual the age of consent in Maui is Sixteen (fifteen if you count the year in the womb)…"

But. Yeh. No.

We did touristy things, and extreme sports things, and other grown-up things, like,

Drink! Drink! Drink! Drink! Drink!

KAHEKILI. Da drink be pink! I do not drink any kine pinky drinkie.

JESSIEE. It's just champagne, God, you're so fifteen.

KAHEKILI. It's li'dat? Kay den.

(Drinks.)

Haw. Dis nasty. Taste like rotten soda, but jus' pink.

JESSIEE. Few sips later –

KAHEKILI. Da waterman, y'know? Da waterman, da waterman, Duke Kahanamoku, Tom Blake, Roger Erikson! My bruddas! Faddas! Idols. Jessiee dey be da Gods a da ocean! Jessiee, watch, neh, soon I be da God a da, somet'ing. Or everyt'ing.

GUIDEBOOK. Boasting total mastery of all oceanic endeavors, the revered waterman can fish, dive, surf, windsurf, kayak, bodysurf, interpret complex weather data, and save the odd drowning man, every now and then. If need be, he can survive entirely on self-harvested ocean bounty, spearing his food from the nearby reefs.

KAHEKILI. I am mini waterman, I know da ocean, she know me, but we da kine y'know, not yet really know, neh? Haw my fadda, he know da ocean, he da kine da any kine bout da ocean, but li'dat he go he go he go, like, neva he know da ocean, like neva he care. He sit deh, wid da small block a wood he mek into smaller block a dis turtle, neh, he know and I know he da smallest buggah on dis island. I wen outgrow my fadda long time ago.

Me, I gon' stay one a da Gods.

GUIDEBOOK. Generally built like a tank and typically soft-spoken (choosing to let his actions do the talking), he's a bit of a loner.

KAHEKILI. An' den da *haole* piece of shit ass leave one dollar fifty-two cent for tip, an' I am fuck you!

Sometimes, da kine, suck, y'know?

I like da watah.

I jus' wanna go watah.

I hate people.

People suck.

You I like.

I like you.

Don't go.

GUIDEBOOK. Watermen fear neither tempest nor shark and rarely head for higher ground.

It's really not for any and every little Hawaiian boy.

KAHEKILI. Marry me.

(Ukulele.)

JESSIEE. Not yet.

KAHEKILI. Marry me.

(Ukulele.)

JESSIEE. We're not there yet.

KAHEKILI. Marry me! Jessiee with two ees. Marry me.

(Ukulele.)

(Ukulele.)

I ask her, marry me.

Marry me, Jessiee with two ees, marry me.

And she say,

And she say,

She say,

JESSIEE. Sure Why not.

KAHEKILI. Yes?!

JESSIEE. No! Yes! I don't know!

KAHEKILI. Why?

JESSIEE. Because you're – and I'm –

Because it's crazy and impossible and are you even allowed to get married?

KAHEKILI. How dat matter? I love you.

JESSIEE. It's a lot more complicated than that.

KAHEKILI. Because why? Jus', I must live wid you fo'eva. Jus' I love you.

JESSIEE. It's not that simple. You're young. You don't understand what it means to –

KAHEKILI. I don't like dis. We tek it back, neh?

GUIDEBOOK. Watermen fear neither tempest nor shark and rarely head for higher ground.

It's really not for any and every little Hawaiian boy.

KAHEKILI. One week wen go by. Learnt t'ings about Jessiee. T'ings people generally learn about new people in one week, maybe little more than dat.

GUIDEBOOK. Jessiee on women's rights:

JESSIEE. Look. If you need to chop off your boobs because it's gonna kill you, it's up to the owner of boob to chop or not chop. But when it comes to the thing in your womb, all of a sudden it's up to the –

what?

KAHEKILI. Did you chop off your, [boobs]?

JESSIEE. Ha, why, did they feel fake to you?

(Awkward.)

KAHEKILI. Look, brah, I was just t'inking, I hope you neva chop off anyt'ing. Life so different after you do that, eh, go chop somet'ing off,

ocean smell different,

rain fall different,

food taste different.

JESSIEE. What did you chop off to know so much?

KAHEKILI. My boobs.

GUIDEBOOK. Jessiee on names:

JESSIEE. – And after the petition is filed, you get a hearing at the civil court, and if it's granted, you get a new social security card, which you need to take to the DMV to get your license changed, also passport, voter regis–

KAHEKILI. All a dat for jus' one more "e"? Dass crazy.

JESSIEE. She thought I needed to feel I don't know special.

KAHEKILI. I t'ink I gon' change my name too. Hello, I am Kahekili with fifty-two "i"s. I am special. I am fifty-two "i"s more special den you. Jessiee's modda say so.

JESSIEE. Jessiee's modda say a lot of things. Jessiee's modda gonna say a whole lot of really pissed off things when Jessiee gets back on the grid.

KAHEKILI. Yah? When Jessiee doin' dat?

JESSIEE. When she sells all her dope.

GUIDEBOOK. Jessiee on family relationships:

JESSIEE. I mean, I love her, she's my best friend, but sometimes, my mom she's such a fucking loser, you know what I mean? Hello, you have cancer, you have no insurance, maybe call your only child about it so we can do something before they take your legs away?

Cut to: four surgeries later, she's lame, I'm bankrupt, both survived to tell the tale of how you wish you hadn't.

KAHEKILI. Where's your fadda?

JESSIEE. Who knows. Who cares. Where's your mom?

(He shrugs.)

KAHEKILI. I t'ink one modda is bettah den one fadda. I wish I had one, even if she one loser.

I would trade my loser fadda for a loser modda anyday.

JESSIEE. I could be your loser mom.

KAHEKILI. I t'ink you too old to be my modda.

JESSIEE. Ha, them fightin' words, brah?

KAHEKILI. You know, if you my modda, I mus' go wid when you leave.

JESSIEE. To Akron?

KAHEKILI. To anywheh. In Hawaii, the son mus' protect his family. Wheh you go, I come wid.

JESSIEE. Maybe. That would be nice.

Although, you wouldn't last very long. Akron is landlocked.

KAHEKILI. What's dat?

JESSIEE. No water. Just land.

(A phone rings.)

GUIDEBOOK. *(As hotel bellboy.)* Excuse me ma'am you have a call awaiting you at the front desk.

(No.)

JESSIEE. What next? What next? Mountain! Can we go up the mountain? Can we bike up the mountain? Laugh my ass off I would die of asphyxiation within the first mile. AHHHHH who the fuck cares. I love this fucking place.

KAHEKILI. I like her talk, her excited talk, eh.

(A phone rings.)

GUIDEBOOK. *(As hotel bellboy.)* For you, ma'am. The gentleman says it is urgent?

(No.)

JESSIEE. Read me something? I don't know, anything, like read the menu. I just fucking love your accent.

Li'dat, bruh!

KAHEKILI. Me an' her talk so different,

but li'dat, like pingpong game, neh,

she go I go she go I go, li'dat, like bam bam bam bam,

so easy so quick so fun I neva know talk so much joy.

I talk wid her and I say t'ings I would neva say.

I do t'ings I neva do neva done.

(A phone rings.)

GUIDEBOOK. *(As hotel bellboy.)* Family emergency, ma'am. Are you sure you would like to decline?

KAHEKILI. I do da t'ings an' I t'ink dis da most stupid t'ing
    I eva done,
    tekin' pictures readin' books,
    drinkin' some stupid drinks like I my fadda or what,
    driving up da mountain fo' see da fuckin' sunrise I
    know I can see bigger an' warmer riding da breaks on
    my own.
    Ho, dis boy not see his board fo' like da whole week.
    Da whole week, my board dryin' up against da wall,
    an' I don't even miss it.
    Not even.

    (JESSIEE *leaves with phone.*)

    So when she go, dass good.
    Yah?
    She go back fo' her grid, I go back fo' my board,
    dis pingpong all dis shit, jus' some fun dass it.
    Dass all.
    No way I leave da ocean, da breaks, da dream of
    waterman, fo' dis pingpong talk dat mek me not me?
    No way I leave my board my Maui, fo' go live wid Jessiee
    on her grid wheh deh stay no ocean?
    Fo' go live wid dis dream lady who hate da watah love
    da mountains.
    Even if she ask,
    Even if she like wanna be my wife my family,
    Dass jus' *lolo*,
    Right?

JESSIEE. Hi, hey. Sorry about that.

KAHEKILI. Everyt'ing good?

JESSIEE. Sure, yeh. Just um, something back home,

KAHEKILI. Home?

JESSIEE. Not, I'm, home. Stuff. Things. I think I have to
    leave this –

KAHEKILI. Na nah na nah na nah na nah, da international police, find you out, neh? Haw, I tole you Jessiee wid two ees, you / gonna get buss up,

JESSIEE. What? No it's not – it's not / funny, stop it Kahekili, I'm not kidding.

KAHEKILI. Tole you about dose credit card trails, neh?

JESSIEE. What the hell are you – will you please –

KAHEKILI. Now dey come at you, we gotta swim now, we gotta swim away, yeh? I'll / save you, I'll save you, Jessiee wid two –

JESSIEE. Are you drunk I said shut the fuck up!

Sorry.

Just, something just fucking –

No more [sad things].

Hey, let's do something different.

KAHEKILI. Kay.

JESSIEE. Let's go somewhere crazy. Like way way way. Let's go up the cliff. Black Rock!

KAHEKILI. I climb up Black Rock every odda day, dass not da somewhere crazy. But if you want, we go climb up first t'ing tomorrow.

JESSIEE. No right now.

Like, now, this moment.

KAHEKILI. Jessiee it's midnight.

JESSIEE. Yeh I know. Like I said, crazy!

I wanna make love to you in the dark on the jagged rocks of the blackest cliff –

BOY. It's like all you ever wanna do now.

Sometimes I'm sorry we discovered sex.

KAHEKILI. You can not go up deh in dis dark, Jessiee. It is illegal. It uh da kine too dangerous, neh?

JESSIEE. Stop being such a fifteen-year-old.

BOY. We could run away?

KAHEKILI. I don't know Jessiee,

BOY. We could run away some place far, like Robinson Crusoe, to an island,

KAHEKILI. I t'ink maybe da better t'ing, go tomorrow morning. Come now.

JESSIEE. No, I really need to,

BOY. Jessie!

KAHEKILI. Jessiee, da whole week, you neva even dip one toe in da watah, now you go up da cliff surrounded all by da sea? Try t'ink t'rough what you gon' do befo' we pull ourselves in fo' sumt'ing *lolo*, yah?

JESSIEE. Okay fine, you puss out, I'll climb up by myself.

KAHEKILI. Kay den, you go you go, kay, shoots, go yourself, fine, you t'ink I care? You go you go, go knock your head open some place stupid in da dark by yourself. Jessiee.

(She's gone.)

BOY. Jessie!

KAHEKILI. Jessiee?

BOY. Jessie! Jessie!

JESSIEE. I'm climbing this cliff right now.
Needs a lot of concentration, lot, of, pep, good things good thoughts.

BOY. Jessie!

JESSIEE. I am in Maui, all the way in Maui, I am happy, no more sad things. No more sad things!

BOY. Jessie!

JESSIEE. Happy happy happy.

BOY. Jessie!

JESSIEE. Eye of the beholder.

BOY. Jessie!

JESSIEE. Oh my god what!

BOY. How?

JESSIEE. What you mean how, I don't know how, I was knocked out for the whole process.

BOY. Jessie.

JESSIEE. Mom.

BOY. You told her?!

JESSIEE. She found the sonogram. She booked the, thing.

BOY. When?

JESSIEE. Yesterday.

BOY. Is it gone, the whole thing?

JESSIEE. No just the odd leg and arm of course the whole thing!

BOY. Why did you do it.

JESSIEE. Benji, come on now we weren't gonna –

BOY. No, you weren't gonna. I had a say, I had a right, I had – I was gonna learn girl hula, You can't kill someone and be –

JESSIEE. I didn't kill anyone! It was gonna kill me!

BOY. You can't kill someone and be done with it.
They become something else, they become stars, air bubbles,

JESSIEE. Those are stories, Benjamin, Oh my god,

BOY. They become something else and we won't know him he won't know us, like Arcas never knew Callisto, and we'll meet one day, and he's gonna shoot us without ever knowing,

JESSIEE. It's just a myth Benji. You can't expect me to give up my life for a myth.

BOY. You gave up my child for SATs.

JESSIEE. That's not fair. It's not that simple.
You're young. You don't understand what it means to have a life.

BOY. Do you?
Goodbye, Jessie.

> (**BOY** *leaves.*)

JESSIEE. The things you lose
sometimes
stay.

The scar,

the stump,

the phantom limb,

the the the not-there-anymore-ness of it becomes a hole and it stays,

– time! They say time helps but actually you know what, it doesn't this is what time does,

time

creates other crap other stumps scars,

piles new sad on to old sad,

you fake forget about the old sad – like pain distraction, slapping your face makes you forget about the tummy ache for a bit kind of thing?

KAHEKILI. Jessiee!

JESSIEE. But all of the things, all of the sad things,

KAHEKILI. Jessiee!

JESSIEE. They stay.

Pool,

flood over,

into some terrifying ocean of lost things.

GUIDEBOOK.

KA'ANAPALI

KAHEKILI. There she was.

JESSIEE. But we ignore this ocean.

GUIDEBOOK.

KA'ANAPALI

KAHEKILI. Tiny girl at tip a da cliff,

JESSIEE. Look away and hope.

GUIDEBOOK.

WHERE THE WAVES ARE YOUNG AND FREE

KAHEKILI. Jessiee!

JESSIEE. Hope, maybe the sad thing will drown and die in your ocean.

KAHEKILI. Jessiee, come down fo' me, neh?

JESSIEE. But it doesn't.

GUIDEBOOK.

    KA'ANAPALI

JESSIEE. *(To* **GUIDEBOOK.***)* Stop.

      *(***GUIDEBOOK** *stops singing.)*

KAHEKILI. Okay, I'm coming deh.

JESSIEE. It grows, waiting.

KAHEKILI. Wait, okay? I'm coming deh.

JESSIEE. Waiting 'til you're on a cliff surrounded by the sea.

KAHEKILI. Full moon tonight, you not gon' win da breaks, Jessiee,

JESSIEE. Leaving your sick mom coz you're mad at her,

KAHEKILI. It gon' for sure break you, neh?

JESSIEE. Mad at her for making you do things you weren't sure you wanted to do, for getting sick for leaving,

KAHEKILI. Jessiee!

JESSIEE. Mad coz

    they say it's better to be mad,

    coz a new sad will make all the old sad feel new all over again.

KAHEKILI. She turn her face fo' da watah an',

JESSIEE. All this water, I smell all this ocean,

KAHEKILI. I know what come next, I know,

JESSIEE. And I see this boy calling, climbing,

KAHEKILI. I climb da rocks, I climb dees rocks I climb fucking every odda day,

    but da breaks, been over da rocks, mek dem slippery,

JESSIEE. But all I could think,

KAHEKILI. I gon' lose her,

JESSIEE. The only thought I can think is,

KAHEKILI. Don't lose her, don't lose her Kahekili, Jessiee!

JESSIEE. No More.

KAHEKILI. I'm here, Jessiee.

JESSIEE. Just, no more.

KAHEKILI. I came fo' you, right?

JESSIEE. You do not get to run away from this any more.

KAHEKILI. No!

    (A leap.)

GUIDEBOOK.

    GIRL MET A BOY
    SHOWED HIM THE WORLD
    OFFERED HER HANDS TO HOLD IN THE SWIRL
    HE MESSED UP HER BED
    EAGER, HE SAID
    "ALL OF MY UNIVERSE IS HERE IN YOUR FACE
    LET ME
    KNOW YOUR EYES, WARM AS THE SUN
    MOLD YOUR SECRETS, DEEP AS YOUR HEART
    TRACE YOUR LIPS, TILL NIGHT TURNS TO MORNING
    DON'T NEED A LOT
    LET ME BE PART OF YOUR BODY"

    BOY MET A GIRL
    GAVE HER THE STARS
    OFFERED THE MOON, VENUS AND MARS
    SHE MESSED UP HIS BED,
    SOFTLY SHE SAID,
    "ALL OF MY UNIVERSE IS HERE IN YOUR PALMS
    LET ME
    KNOW YOUR FINGERS, SOFT AS THE SUN
    MOLD YOUR FISTS, BIG AS YOUR HEART
    TRACE YOUR ARMS, TILL NIGHT TURNS TO MORNING
    DON'T NEED THE STARS,
    LET ME BE PART OF YOUR –"

    (A loud splash, a body thrown into a mass of water.)

KAHEKILI. Dis dream,

    dis lady,

    da waves da breaks dey eat up dis lady.

    But dis time I fly after her, I can ass da ocean fo' give lady back, dis time not dream,

dis da real t'ing,

JESSIEE. Frogs, thousands of them,

but they were dead, taken care of,

and there's this one little frog, cute even, singing to me, lulling me to Maui,

it was a good feeling. It was a good dream.

When the nurse woke me up, he was like, I'm sorry but you can't sleep on the cafeteria floor,

while eyeballing this guidebook that had been serving as a headrest.

I'm like, dude, my mom's on her fourth surgery, our entire life savings belong to you now,

I'm allowed to borrow a past-season guidebook to lean on while I fucking nap on whichever fucking surface I fucking choose to nap on, no?

I didn't say that.

I wiped my drool, mumbled something about I'm sorry I'm tired and went back to Mom.

Back to Mom. Just Mom and me.

KAHEKILI. Jus' me and da ocean.

I swim I swim I swim,

I stroke and stroke and stroke.

It's like da ocean, she jealous of my pingpong talk an' decide, out odda fucking blue she gon' tek her again.

I look I look I look fo' da head, I know dis head, I seen dis head ten thousand times befo'.

JESSIEE. I was reading to her, from this guidebook.

I was reading to her, about the sunset luaus by the beach where you can learn to hula,

both boy hula and girl hula, and

I got hungry, just really really hungry.

KAHEKILI. Jessiee!

JESSIEE. The surgery was going to be in a couple hours,

Mom says I should go get something to eat, that she would be fine for a while.

KAHEKILI. Jessiee!

JESSIEE. The surgery won't start for a couple hours.

KAHEKILI. I swim I swim I swim,
I stroke and stroke and stroke.

JESSIEE. So I went for a corndog.
Got in the car, drove down the road, looking for a sign, that said,

KAHEKILI. Jessiee!

JESSIEE. I don't know, corndog,

KAHEKILI. No head, no head, ocean bitch fuckin' eat her up eat her up.

JESSIEE. And somehow I'm at the airport.

KAHEKILI. I look fo' da head, I know dis head,

JESSIEE. Found a sign, destination: Maui.

KAHEKILI. Seen dis head ten thousand times befo'.

JESSIEE. Not exactly corndog, but I felt like, that's where I might go, where I might –

KAHEKILI. I swim I swim I –

JESSIEE. Where I might fill my craving,

KAHEKILI. But my arms, my legs,

JESSIEE. It was her fourth surgery.

KAHEKILI. So tired. I wish,

JESSIEE. They didn't need me. They've never needed me.

KAHEKILI. I wish, still da watah stay!

JESSIEE. So I called Mom,
said Mom I'm going to Maui.
She asked for some chocolate covered macadamia nuts,
I bought the ticket and jumped on the flight.

KAHEKILI. So I say,
ocean you win.
I roll onto one small rock under da cliff.

I pick one star an' I pray to da buggah,
Please. Let Jessiee come to shore.

JESSIEE. Funny story, when I got that call, the only thing I
could think about was, so, what do I do with all those
chocolate covered macadamia nuts in my hotel room.
I'm barely conscious in the water, and still I'm like,
macadamia nuts.

I should give them to Kahekili. Or maybe he hates
macadamia nuts. Wow, I'm never gonna know if this
kid liked macadamia nuts or not.

KAHEKILI. Den like a miracle,
psst psst blink blink,
da star show me,
Jessiee's head up an' down up an' down,
Jessiee's body over an' under da breaks,
I know right den, dat da shape odda body not breathing,
an' no t'ink, no plan a action,
I jus' fall straight back into dis watah again.

> (*A loud splash, a body thrown into a mass of water.*)
>
> (**GUIDEBOOK** *begins to underscore this moment with the previously introduced Hawaiian song, while* **KAHEKILI** *embraces* **JESSIEE**, *lifts her in his arms. Takes her to shore.*)
>
> (*A long kiss.*)
>
> (*Like the first time they met.*)
>
> (*And then the kiss turns into something else, something more desperate.*)
>
> (*When the song comes to the end of a verse:*)
>
> (**JESSIEE** *starts, chokes up water.*)

KAHEKILI. Kay den. You stay alright, stay alright, jus' spit all
da ocean out, spit it out,
Dass good, all a da ocean. Spit her out. Spit, kay den.
Kay.

(**KAHEKILI** *collapses on the sand.*)

(*Lots of breathing. Breathing.*)

(*They lie there, staring up at the sky.*)

JESSIEE. Do you like macadamia nuts?

(**KAHEKILI** *shakes his head slowly.*)

I'm leaving. Soon. Akron. I have these nuts, I don't need. I thought if you wanted them you could have them.

KAHEKILI. Jessiee,

JESSIEE. But you don't like them, which doesn't mean anything,

KAHEKILI. Jessiee.

JESSIEE. You can not like something and still have them.

KAHEKILI. Marry me.

JESSIEE. …

KAHEKILI. Marry me.

JESSIEE. …

KAHEKILI. Jessiee wid two ees, marry me.

JESSIEE. No.

KAHEKILI. I love you.

BOY. I love you.

JESSIEE. Not that simple.

KAHEKILI. Jus', I must live wid you fo'eva. Jus' I love you. Simple.

JESSIEE. You're young. You don't understand what it means to have a life,

BOY. Do you?

KAHEKILI. I'm all buss up, Jessiee. I can't pingpong you right now.

Jus' I want fo' live wid you fo'eva. Don't leave. Easy.

BOY. We could run away? Like Robinson Crusoe.

JESSIEE. You are fifteen. I am thirty-two.

KAHEKILI. I look thirty-two. You look fifteen. Without IDs, people t'ink I tek you on a ride, neh?

BOY. We could go to Hawaii.

KAHEKILI. Jessiee. You jus' fly off da cliff in da midnight. I jus' wen save your life.

We can do anyt'ing. Jessiee, we can do any kine we want.

BOY. I could catch things in the sea, teach Jasmin how to hula,

KAHEKILI. Marry me.

JESSIEE. You are fifteen. I am thirty-two.

KAHEKILI. Da number of years lived on earth means da number of years lived on earth.

Not'ing more. You trippin' over da kine sex.

JESSIEE. Kahekili.

KAHEKILI. No no, listen fo' me.

We had sex. But also we eat togedda, we have pingpong talk togedda, we get scared about each odda head be up down in da sea togedda, dass family,

Jessiee wid two ees, we already family, see? We already married.

JESSIEE. You're good at this.

KAHEKILI. I'm good at a lot a t'ings. Marry me.

JESSIEE. I can't.

KAHEKILI. Because why!

JESSIEE. Because you are fifteen. And I'm, not.

(The stars are, many.)

GUIDEBOOK. *(As Airport PA.)* Passengers of US Airways Flight 17 bound for Cleveland with stops in Seattle and Atlanta, the departure gate has been changed to 30B. Also, there will be a slight delay to departure due to inclement weather. Thank you for your patience.

JESSIEE. Do you get people to see you off at the airport?

I don't. Sure, I get rides, I always have bundles of shit,

But we get there, unload bags, then I send the driver on their way, outside the door.

Because,

well,

it's awkward, isn't it?

You know one of you is going to go a very long way and it might be a while till you come back.

And those goodbyes, should be short and sweet. A hug and a peck.

Otherwise, it becomes an hour of staring at the crap coffee trying not to cry,

or an hour of talking about anything and everything trying to cram in every last bit of information about yourself into that other person's brain.

The crap thing is tho,

When you do successfully send the driver on their way,

For some reason you still keep hoping,

maybe a miracle will happen,

and they will slide in through the gates, out of breath and completely gross with sweat –

to plant that last final movie airport kiss,

cut to: few months later, they're married to you or something.

GUIDEBOOK. *(As Airport PA.)* Passengers of US Airways Flight 17 bound for Cleveland with stops in Seattle and Atlanta, the departure gate has been changed forever. Also, there will be an infinite delay to departure due to something or another. Stay a while, have a Mai Tai, get married and have babies, build a house, build a shrine of hands,

JESSIEE. They never do come back.

And it is because you sent them away.

And whether you believe you did the right thing or not, the law, the petitions, the picketlines, the shaking heads, the good-girl police in every well-meaning advice giver, crowds your choice with so much noise, and you dare not ever voice what it meant, what it cost you, to send them away, the way that you did.

Meanwhile, the fiction miracle loops on in your mind's movie.

KAHEKILI. Strange, fo' have some odda bugga in da head.
   Strange, li'dat in your chest or some stuff.
   Not pain, or li' "haaaak! I no can live no more!!"
   but different.

   Ocean smell different,
   rain fall different,
   food taste different,

   An' I not even chop off my boob.

   When Jessiee go, she wen' put da bags in da taxi,
   an' give me one hug, quick kiss on da face, and a whole
   lotta macadamia nuts.
   I wen' turn around an' shoot straight da odda way.
   Li'dat, straight da odda way.
   I jus' wen' tek my board out to Honolua, paddle some,
   nap some, look out at da sky some.
   It's good.
   I'm teaching myself to be jus' happy for her head be
   above watah, neh?
   Maybe one day we gon' meet again,
   maybe we don't,
   but for today it's nice,
   dat she mek me worry.

   (Seat belt on sign "ping.")

   (A goodbye.)

GUIDEBOOK. Mahalo, we hope you enjoyed your stay in
   Maui, Hawaii, one of the most sought after destinations
   on the planet. With over two and half million visitors
   almost every year, we know that you know that Maui is
   the most happiest place to be. Do come back.

End of Play

Girl met a boy

MUSIC AND LYRICS
Hansol Jun

Girl met a boy   Showed him the world
Boy met a girl   Gave her the stars

Of - fered her   hands   to hold in the swirl   He
Of - fered the   moon   ve - nus and mars   She

messed up her bed   Ea - ger, he said   "All of my
messed up his bed   soft-ly she said   "All of my

U-ni-verse is here in your face   let me know your eyes
U-ni verse is here in your palms let me know your fingers

warm as the sun   mold your se-crets,   deep as your
soft as the sun   mold your fi - sts   big as your

heart   Trace your lips,   till night turns to morn-ing don't
heart   Trace your arms,   till night turns to morn-ing don't

need a lot   let me be part of your   bo - dy
need the stars   let me be part of your

D.C. al Coda

(splash)

Ka'anapali (the Vignette)

MUSIC: Hansol Jung
LYRICS: Jongbin Jung

B

Don't miss the sun - rise at Ha-le - a -

E

ka - la

F

We-ather can be un - pre - dict - a - ble

B♭

ten - thou-sand feet a - bove sea lev - el...

Ka'anapali

MUSIC: Hansol Ju
LYRICS: Jongbin Ju

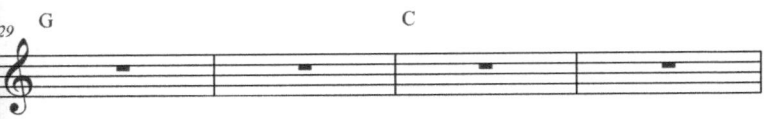

Grab a board and - ride - the - pass - ing - tide -

- Grab a snor - kel - Let - the - worr - ies - slide -

- Ev-ery thing's eas - y - in Ka 'a na pa li

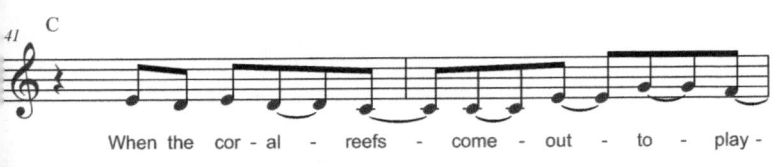

When the cor - al - reefs - come - out - to - play -

- O - cean won - ders bright - ten up the bay

O - f Ka 'a na pa li